The Life We Dream

ISBN: 978-0-9839069-3-3

Cover Concept and Design: JH Glaze
Text Editing: Susan Grimm
First Printing December 2011
Published by MostCool Media Inc.
"Make it interesting. Make it MostCool."

Proudly printed in the United States of America.

First Edition January 2013

10 9 8 7 6 5 4 3 2 1

I want to thank my wife, Susan, for challenging me to write this story despite the fact that my usual subject matter is far from what is contained herein. Not only does she inspire me through her enduring support of my work, she makes me a better person each day. She taught me how to love.

Thank you to my Paranormal Warriors Street Team and my FB Administrators for all you do every day.

Thank you to the bloggers who continue to feature me and the online radio hosts who have interviewed me, some on several occasions.

Thank you to you, the readers and the folks who read my work and take the time to review it. Reviews mean more to us than you can imagine.

Look for other titles by JH Glaze:

The Spirit Box – John Hazard Book I
NorthWest – John Hazard Book II
Send No Angel – John Hazard Book III
The RUNE Series
The Horror Challenge Volume I
The Horror Challenge Volume II
The Horror Challenge Volume III
Forced Intelligence

Available on Amazon.com and other online retailers.

The Life We Dream

"*Even when we are thankful for every gift and the blessings the day may bring, it may never seem to be as good or sweet as the perfect life we dream.*"

~JH Glaze

The Call

Rush hour was not the time to be on the road, and this was not the place to be trapped. Cars on all sides inched past as Jack sat fuming, his right turn signal flashing. He was hoping for some glimmer of humanity to filter through the tinted windows of the exasperated drivers coming up from behind him. Desperate to change lanes before the last half mile of cracked pavement leading up to his exit passed beneath his tires, at long last he saw a gap opening up. Perhaps someone with a heart was giving him the opportunity to move over.

Just as he started to merge into the lane to his right, his phone began to ring. Fumbling with the wheel as he lifted himself from the seat, he reached into the tight back pocket where he kept his phone. By the time he wrangled it free, his window of opportunity had closed and he missed his exit. He pushed the button on the phone, his frustration evident as he answered, "Yeah, this is Jack."

The caller hesitated. "Hello, uh, is this Jack Bailey, the one who graduated from Washington High, class of '89?" It had been a long time since he had heard anyone mention his high school. It piqued his interest enough that, suddenly, it didn't matter so much that he had just missed his exit.

"Yeah, that's me. Whatcha got?" he snapped as he tried to ease into the farthest right lane to get off at the next exit.

"Jack, this is Art Cline. You might not remember me, but..."

"Art, my man! I might be getting older, but I'm not relying on *Depends* yet! How the hell are you? It's been forever." Having an old friend reach out to him suddenly brightened his mood.

"Yeah, uh... I'm doing all right. Guess I can't complain."

"Good! Good! What's going on? I haven't talked to you since our days at Washington. Hey, did you and Sarah ever end up getting together? You know, married and all?"

"Sure did, but sorry to say it didn't turn out so well. Did you know I followed her after she moved away in our junior year? We did a couple years of college together. Yeah, well, we hung in there for about ten years after getting married, tried to have a kid, but it never worked out. We ended up getting a divorce."

Jack felt a twinge as his heart began to beat a little faster. "That's too bad, man. Sorry to hear it. I know how hard you worked to win her away from... I mean... oh... never mind. Yeah, that sucks."

"No, Jack, it's okay. In fact, I met a great woman after that and made her my wife. Things are going pretty well for me now, but Sarah, well, I'm gonna be straight with you. One of the things I hated when we were together was her constant references to the old times back at Washington High. She had a lot of regrets about some decisions she had made, and it was obvious."

"Well, hell, Art, those were good times. I can see why she enjoyed the memories. Life was easy, and we had all the time in the world..."

"No... it's not that. Look, I don't know how to say this. It always bothered me..." He stopped.

Jack came up on his exit and eased onto the off-ramp behind the line of blinking taillights ahead of him. "Divorce is rough, Art. I mean, I never went through it myself but a lot of my friends have... Just a symptom of the world we live in, I guess."

"Yeah, the divorce *was* hard. I had tried everything I could to make her happy, but..." Again, he hesitated.

Jack was growing impatient with his old friend. As he came to the light and made a left to cross back to the opposite flow of traffic, he was ready to get to the point. "Look, Art, I'm not having such a good day so far. You called for a reason, what's up?"

"Sarah. That's why I called. She's in hospice. She's dying, Jack. Ovarian cancer. They say she has only days, hell, maybe hours left." He paused before repeating, "That's why I called."

Jack was stunned. This was the woman he had always claimed was the love of his life, and she was dying? He felt sick to his stomach. "Hang on a second, Art."

Instead of maneuvering into the turning lane to get back on the freeway, he dropped the phone on the passenger seat and made for the right lane, dodging traffic and pulling into the first business entrance. The gas station was bustling with cars pulling up to and driving away from the pumps, so he drove over to the side of the building and parked in the first empty space. Only then did he pick up his phone again. "Are you still there?"

"Yeah. Sorry to drop the news on you like that. I know how much you cared for her, and…"

"No, I appreciate you calling me. Do you have the address where she is now?"

"Yes, right here."

"Do me a favor and send it to me in a text message. Will you be seeing her today by any chance?"

"Uh, no, man. The wife would shit if she even knew I had this much information. She's always been jealous of Sarah. When we first got together, she used to ask if I was sneaking out to…"

"Can you send me the address, Art? I really would appreciate it."

"Oh, yeah, sure. No problem."

"Great, I'm gonna hang up now, but please don't forget. And, Art, I really appreciate this. I owe you, man."

"Hey, no prob..." Jack pushed the button to disconnect the call.

Memories

Jack stared at the small duffle bag on the bed. He had no idea what he was going to stuff into it. Would he be gone for a few days or a week? Maybe longer? He had no idea. What he did know was that he had at least five hundred miles to drive, and he needed to get on the road. Every minute he delayed was another breath that could be Sarah's last.

"Pull yourself together, man." He told himself. His mind was cluttered with memories as he recalled the first time he had met her.

~~~~~~~~~~~~~~~~~

In the fall of 1976, on the first day of school, his mother had stooped down to give him a reassuring hug just outside the door of his kindergarten classroom. He was crying as she kissed him on the cheek. With one last squeeze, she wiped his tears with a crumpled tissue she pulled from her pocket and took him by the shoulders.

"Jack, honey, don't cry. It's going to be a lot of fun. Look at all of the new friends you will get to play with. I'll bet some of these kids will become your friends for life. It's exciting, honey, to be starting your first day of school. You're a big boy now, you can do this." With that, she kissed him again and, as she stood up, turned him toward the classroom. She gave him an encouraging push toward his smiling teacher. When he turned back to wave to her, she was already gone.

With tears still streaking his cheeks, he shuffled his way into the room to begin his education. Right away, he was given a nametag and assigned a seat at one of the tables according to his last name. At first, his mind was taken with worry that his mother would forget him. Then, as the day went on, he became more interested in the children around him. Eventually, the games they played helped him to relax and enjoy himself. By the time his first day ended, he was torn between wanting to stay and play with his new friends and going home with his mom.

On the drive home, she asked him about his day. With a great deal of excitement, he related everything that had happened. When he came to the end of his tale, she looked at him and smiled. "See, honey, some things in life are only scary when they're not familiar. We should never be afraid to try new things, or we will miss out on a lot of life."

~~~~~~~~~~~~~~~~~~

Carefully packing for the trip, Jack gathered a few things from the bathroom. He smiled as he recalled his mother's philosophies. He realized that every time in his life that he had pushed through his natural reluctance, he was always glad he had done so. Of course, there was that one time when he had tried bungee jumping...

All packed now, except for one thing, he checked the locks and made sure that all appliances and electronics were turned off. His heart twitched with a mix of excitement and sorrow as he picked up his keys and a worn out old shoe box from the bed, taking one last look around. He was going to see the love of his life for the first time in more than twenty years, a girl he had truly never forgotten.

He had often fantasized about meeting Sarah again. Such imaginings always ended happily, because *he* had the power to decide how it would end. This time, he knew that reality would hold more pain than joy, yet there was no doubt in his mind that he must make the journey.

Jack locked the door behind him and bounded down the steps toward his car, a vision of her face flashing through his mind. Young and full of life, he saw himself talking to her at a picnic surrounded by a group of friends. It was a time just before she had moved away. "I know how much you love me, Jack," she had told him. "I'm sorry it didn't work out for us, really I am, but we have our whole lives ahead of us. You know what I mean?"

Those were the last words she had spoken to him, and the last time he had seen her in all these years. Once again, he felt the ache of losing her. Opening his car door, he threw his bag and the box on the seat beside him as he got in. He typed his destination into his GPS and selected *Fastest Route* before driving off. In minutes, he was out of his neighborhood and headed to the freeway for the last time today.

Imprint

The second week of kindergarten arrived, and with it a new girl in the class. She cried as her mother explained how she would be back to pick her up at the end of the day. His heart melted for her as he remembered his first day only a week ago. As the class settled into their chairs, he crossed the room and approached her.

It looked as though she had been crying for a while. Her eyes were wet and reddened, and she sniffled and snorted in a vain attempt to control the flow from her runny nose. He paid no attention. It was her green eyes, auburn hair, and the sweet curve of her cheek as it met the corner of her mouth that had captivated him. She smiled as he moved closer, a crooked sweet smile of gratitude, and he noticed she was clutching a handful of tissues as though her life depended on them.

Her mother whispered just before she left the room, "Don't worry, Sarah. It will be fun, you'll see." He took another step closer and, without the least hesitation, offered his arms to her in a comforting hug. "Don't cry, okay? It's not so bad."

Taking her hand, he led her into the room. "Last week, when I cried, my mom told me it would be fun, and it was true."

The flow of tears immediately came to an end, and she smiled again at her new hero. She had made her first new friend but, for him, it went much deeper. He had fallen in love.

~~~~~~~~~~~~~~~~~

Traffic on the freeway was not letting up. The twilight combined with light rain played a role in a fatal four-car pile up that had blocked three lanes of traffic. All the cars inching past the scene slowed to a near stop to get a glimpse of the carnage on their way to wherever they were headed. To Jack, this was maddening. He had been dealing with the rush hour traffic not an hour earlier.

More than a little frazzled, he yelled at the cars ahead of him. "What the hell, people? Haven't you ever seen a car crash?" It was a waste of breath, but at least it gave him a chance to blow off some steam at the delay. He had a friend who needed him, and this was no time to be stuck in traffic.

About an hour later, he was miles away from the city. Now there was enough breathing room between cars to kick it up past the speed limit. He was surprised, however, when he looked at his speedometer and found he had been doing well over ninety mph. He backed off the gas and checked his rearview mirror for flashing blue lights. Relieved, he slowed to just over the limit and pressed the button for cruise control. If he were lucky tonight, the cops would not be out trying to push their quota of tickets for the month. Relaxed again, his mind began to wander again.

~~~~~~~~~~~~~~~~~

First grade seemed perfect to him. Every day, he woke early and got dressed as well as a six-year-old could before skipping down the stairs to the kitchen for breakfast. His mother would set out a couple of boxes of cereal, but he would always check the pantry for his favorite toaster pastry before he could resign himself to a cold bowl of crunch. Whatever he ended up choosing, he would eat as quickly as possible and then head out to wait for the bus.

At school, he and Sarah were inseparable, teaming up whenever possible. During recess, Jack did everything he could to help Sarah win the games that they played, even if it meant that he would lose. At lunchtime, they sat across the table from one another, and he would listen while Sarah talked about anything, or nothing at all. He especially enjoyed the times when there was food on the lunch menu that she disliked. She would pass those things to him because it bothered her to throw anything away. He was always hungry, it seemed.

From that year on, through elementary school, their classmates had chanted, "Jack and Sarah sitting in a tree..." As they had grown closer, all of their friends teased them about getting married someday, but they didn't care. They just smiled and ignored them. Besides, it seemed the right thing to do as far as he was concerned.

~~~~~~~~~~~~~~~~~~

"Huh? What are those kids doing in the back of that truck? It looks like they're holding some kind of sign." He was talking to himself as he sped up to see what they were doing. As he got closer he could make it out. They had written, "Help, our parents are crazy!"

He might have been concerned if they hadn't been laughing. Instead, he blew the horn just to stir things up. He could see their mother turn around and the sign came down as she dealt with her little pranksters. That made him smile. He remembered doing things like that on long road trips when he was a kid. It was usually a trucker that would get him busted when they blew their horn.

Summer of Change

Between sixth and seventh grade, Sarah had gone to visit her grandmother in some other state. She might as well have traveled to a foreign country as far as he had been concerned. When she told him of the trip, she promised it would only be for a couple of weeks.

"Don't worry," she assured him, "we'll see each other again soon." Two weeks later, he began to anticipate her return, but she did not call. He hadn't heard anything at all from her. By the third week, he was worried. Finally, he called.

"Oh, she's fine, Jack," her mother answered. "She's having so much fun that she asked if she could stay another week. Actually, we decided to let her stay for the rest of the summer."

He hung up the phone without saying goodbye. The pain in his stomach had made him feel like he was about to be sick. It was not like any flu he'd ever experienced. He wanted to lie down on his bed, but decided to tell his mother first. She tried to rule out the possibility of food poisoning, asking when he had started to feel bad.

"Aw, I was worried about Sarah so I called her house. She hasn't come home from her grandmother's house. Now her mom told me she is staying all summer. When I was hanging up the phone, I felt like I was gonna throw up!"

His mother smiled. "Honey, you aren't sick... well, at least, I don't think you have a bug. You're just lovesick." She rubbed his back. "You feel bad because you miss her so much, right?" When he nodded, she assured him, "It happens sometimes when you are in love. You are separated a long time, and you actually start to feel pain, like an ache that you can't relieve with medicine. Sorry, honey. There's no medicine for that."

"Mom! I'm not 'in love'." He always squirmed as any boy his age would when the word, 'love,' was mentioned, especially by his mother. "I just miss her real bad."

"Okay, honey. Missing her 'real bad' can make you feel that way, too. You'll be fine, you'll see."

He sighed, "But it seems like she's been gone forever!"

"Maybe we should sign you up for some swimming lessons. That might take your mind off Sarah for a while."

By the end of the summer, he was distracted enough by the activities his mother had arranged for him that he stopped feeling so alone. Still, he wondered if she was ever coming back. The night before school started, he had trouble sleeping. He had waited a long time for the reunion. He wondered if she would be as happy to see him as he was to see her.

Arriving at school, he hurried to his new homeroom, but she was not there. All day he gazed out the window watching to see whether her mother was going to bring her in late. Sarah never arrived. That night, he tried calling her.

"Hello, may I speak to Sarah, please?"

"Is this Jack? How are you? How was your summer?" Her mother had such a sweet, friendly voice, but he was quite eager to talk to Sarah.

"It was fine, ma'am. Is Sarah there?"

"Yes she is, honey, but she's asleep. I guess she picked up a bug just before she left her grandmother's house. I'll tell her you called, okay?"

"Uh... will she be at school tomorrow?" He had to know if he would see her.

"I think so, Jack, if she feels better. She's looking forward to it."

"Okay then, thank you." He had forgotten to say goodbye again. She was excited about going back to school! That is what he had wanted to hear.

~~~~~~~~~~~~~~~~~

Halfway to his destination, Jack pulled off the highway. He stopped at one of those large truck stops with multiple fast food restaurants, ordered a burger, and sat down in the lobby to eat it. The break from the drive had come as a relief. He was tired. Watching the people around him come and go, he noticed a teenage girl with long auburn hair walking in. Something about the way she brushed the hair from her eyes triggered his memories once again.

~~~~~~~~~~~~~~~~~

The next day, he had gotten off the bus and raced down the hallway to his homeroom. He burst through the door looking toward his desk hoping to see her in her usual seat. His heart sank when he saw the empty desk. Then, when he turned to check the front of the room, there she stood, talking with the teacher. He was unable to hold back. Throwing his backpack on his desk chair, he ran to greet her. "Sarah!"

Sarah seemed completely oblivious and he stopped in his tracks. This was an entirely different girl from the one he'd said goodbye to last spring. Like one of the flowers in his mother's garden, his friend had grown and blossomed. The spindly girl was now a young woman. It was breathtaking. She was taller, for sure, but what caught him off guard were the budding breasts pressed against her blouse. She was more beautiful to him than ever. Suddenly shy, he tried to pull himself together.

"Hey, Sarah!" He choked out the words as his voice cracked. Sounding a little like a frightened

goose, he was embarrassed at his changing voice.

"Oh hi, Jack." She sounded so casual. "I have so many stories to tell you. I had a wonderful time at my Nana's. We can talk later."

"Oh. Yeah, uh, okay, maybe later, uh, like when the bell rings?"

"Sure. Maybe then."

He had walked to his seat still clinging to the hope that nothing was changed between them. In the days and weeks to follow, however, he would discover that everything had changed. The way she carried herself, the way she dressed, and even the way she spoke had gone through a transformation. In fact, every time she inserted something about her summer vacation into their conversation, he was painfully reminded of his long lonely summer.

As the holidays approached, he began to feel more desperate. He wanted to be more than just one of Sarah's friends, but he didn't know how to approach her. What used to be so simple was now so awkward. Finally, he asked his friend, Tony, to talk to Sarah for him. He wanted to know if there was something she wasn't telling him, and he wanted to know if there was any chance that she would say yes to "going steady" with him.

As far as he was concerned, his instructions to Tony were perfectly clear. He was to play it cool and gather some facts. That was his mission and *nothing more. It was that easy. He could have never predicted how his friend would fail him.*

Tony had called Sarah that Friday night while Jack waited for his call. However, late on Saturday night, he had yet to hear from Tony. On Sunday morning, he had decided to check in with his friend for a report. Tony's mother dropped a bomb that he never saw coming. Tony was not at home. He had gone to church with Sarah and her parents!

Let's Be Friends

Food fight! The girl with the auburn hair was there to meet some friends, and they were beginning to heat things up. The first volley came with fries raining down on the other side of the room. Retaliation came in waves of chicken nuggets and the spray from ketchup packets. By the time the security guard entered the room, the battle was just about over. The kids were out of food and the resulting mess was more on the girls than the décor of the restaurant. With the excitement at an end, Jack returned to his thoughts.

~~~~~~~~~~~~~~~~~

On Monday morning, he had noticed Sarah deep in conversation with one of her friends. Highly animated, and with frequent bursts of girlish laughter, they seemed to be enjoying themselves. He didn't feel like interrupting. He just slumped down in his seat. When she finally came over to sit down, she greeted him enthusiastically. "Hi, Jack! Do anything fun over the weekend?"

"Naw, nothing really, just hung out in my room." He couldn't wait for her to bring it up. "So, did you talk to Tony?"

The smile slipped from her face and she flushed a bright red. Jack recognized that look, and he knew he wasn't going to like what she was about to say. "Yeah, he called me on Friday. We talked a long time, like forever! Did you know that his parents came here from Spain?"

"Not really." His felt his heart sinking.

"Yeah, they're from Barcelona. His dad got a job here a couple of years ago. Before that, they lived in New York City, and that's where he was born. I guess that's why he doesn't have an accent. Did you know he can speak Spanish?"

"No, I..." He felt like his head would explode. He speaks Spanish? He never speaks Spanish! Right then, he wanted to find Tony and kick the Spanish right out of him.

"Isn't it cool?" Sarah sounded way too excited about this. "His mother taught him, so when he goes to Spain, he can talk to his grandparents."

Jack hadn't wanted to hear any of this. What he wanted to know was what Tony had said, why he had gone to church with her, and what exactly was going on. He didn't have to wait much longer. She was about to tear his heart out and throw it on the floor. Sarah leaned toward him and whispered, "Tony asked me to be his girlfriend. I said yes." She waited for his

response and, when none came, she asked him,
"Jack? What d'ya think?"

~~~~~~~~~~~~~~~~~

He tossed the trash from his meal into the bin. It was time to get back on the road. Stopping first in the men's room, he splashed his face with cold water. He needed to stay alert. As he got back into the car, he checked his GPS. He took a deep breath as the big yellow numbers screamed, *120.5 miles.*

As far as he was concerned, it was taking way too long to reach the woman he had always dreamt of sharing his life with. She was leaving this world forever, and he needed to see her one last time. He pressed down on the gas pedal, accelerating to ninety. He was never one to push the speed limit to excess. Until tonight, that is.

Midnight

Jack rubbed his eyes to relieve the burning sensation that came from staring at the road for such a long time. During the entire trip, he had travelled without any music or any other distraction. He was tired, and he needed something to help him stay awake. Turning the radio on, he tuned in to some classic rock.

Journey's "Don't Stop Believing" was playing, and Steve Perry was full into the chorus. However, even that hopeful message could not prevent him from occasionally nodding off. A few times, he scared himself as the car edged off the road, rattling as the tires passed over rough concrete. He swore to himself that he would stop at the next exit and splash some more cold water on his face. Some strong coffee would help him stay on schedule. Despite his determination, his mind began to drift again.

~~~~~~~~~~~~~~~~~

How devastating it had been to learn that his nows former friend was Sarah's new boyfriend. He was barely able to keep his mind focused at school. When he was at home, things were even worse. It seemed that every song he heard, or any television show he watched, reminded him of her. Suddenly, every female character on TV was named Sarah! He switched to watching his favorite horror flicks, but in every one of them, there was a Sarah. Even the chick in the Terminator movie was Sarah Connor.

In their younger years, he assumed they would be together forever. Sarah had written it on little scraps of pink paper that he had saved in the old shoebox he kept tucked away in his closet. He had trouble getting used to the idea that he had lost her now. Several times, he tried talking to her about it. He had wanted to tell her how he'd asked Tony to talk to her, but he realized how ridiculous it would sound. Of course, she would ask him why he hadn't talked to her himself.

After several months, as things often go, Tony and Sarah had broken up. Their brief relationship was somewhat stormy, full of disagreements and spats. Sarah was still recovering from the break up when he decided to approach her.

"Hey, Sarah, how's it going?"

"Fine. At least as good as it can be right now, considering I feel like crap."

"I hear ya. Well... so... this week being homecoming and all..."

"You weren't planning on asking me to the dance were you, Jack?"

"Uh, well, yeah. I was, kinda."

"Look, we've known each other for, like, forever." *She held up her hand to indicate that he shouldn't go on.* *"I don't think I can ever be your girlfriend. I mean it's like you're my brother or something. It just doesn't feel right."*

Jack was crushed, but made one last attempt. "But..."

"No, Jack. Let's just be friends. Is that okay?"

He tried very hard not to let his face show the injury she'd inflicted upon his heart as her words rang in his ears. His efforts had been in vain, though, and he felt the heat radiating in his cheeks as his face cycled through ten shades of red.

Covering, he had bluffed, "Yeah, I know..." Swallowing hard then, "but you don't have to go as my girlfriend. We could just go to the dance, have fun, like the old days."

"Maybe, if I didn't already have plans," Sarah sighed, "but Mike already asked me. I said yes, Jack, so I'll be going with him."

~~~~~~~~~~~~~~~~~

The deer was standing in the middle of the road, and by the time he realized it, Jack was right up on it. Fortunately, his reflexes were operating well ahead of him. With a combination of braking and turning the wheel, he narrowly missed the animal. Pulling over to the side of the road, he took a few minutes to allow the adrenalin to subside. It was a close call for sure. He was lucky he hadn't hit the thing.

Although he decided to drive a bit slower, before he knew it he was back up to ninety. He eased his foot off the gas until the speedometer slipped back to sixty-seven and pushed the button for cruise control once more. Now he wouldn't be tempted to go any faster. He would just maintain a safer constant speed.

The near disaster caused Jack a moment of reflection. He considered some regrets, things he might have done differently, or maybe not at all. Then pushing himself back in his seat, he returned to thoughts of Sarah.

~~~~~~~~~~~~~~~~~~

During their junior year of high school, he had tried to heal his hurt by dating other girls. Honestly, he was certain he would eventually forget about Sarah, but his heart did not agree. He was not able to maintain any other relationship. Every time he encountered Sarah in homeroom or while passing through the halls, his heartstrings tightened like piano wires. The fires of his heart burned for her alone.

Fortune taunted him that year. He had been assigned as her biology partner. They actually worked well as a team. He did all the cutting and dissecting, and she documented the results. It worked well, except that Sarah had trouble watching the procedure and the smell of formaldehyde had a tendency to make her sick to her stomach.

He never guessed that she was keeping a secret. At the end of the school year, her family would move several hundred miles away. Her father had been transferred, and like a thief in the night, he stole Sarah away.

The next September, on the first day of school, he had discovered that he had been assigned to the very seat that for twelve years had been occupied by his true love. He had been moved forward to fill the gap created by her absence, but he had no idea what had happened to her.

At first, he feared that something terrible had happened to her. One of her friends finally informed him of the disturbing news. She was gone, moved away. Although he was relieved to learn that she was alive and well, he shivered from the feeling that a part of him had died that day.

Not Again

Jack rubbed his eyes and tried to shake off the fatigue. Around 3:30 a.m., his GPS indicated that he was just four miles from his destination. He was filled with great anticipation at the prospects of reuniting with Sarah. He shifted in his seat and tried to relax. His legs were aching and his arms were tired, but he was compelled to push on.

Glancing at the GPS again, then back to the road, he saw something flash in the corner of his eye. The buck was airborne before he had time to react. Vaulting four feet off the pavement, it began a slow motion leap across the front of the car. Jack watched in horror as the large deer slammed into the windshield. He jammed his foot onto the brake while glass sprayed across his face. The injured deer kicked and jerked, striking him in the face.

White smoke trailed from the tires as he locked the brakes and rubber tore at the pavement. There were no other cars in sight as he skidded down a slight embankment, then up the other side and into a stand of trees. With blood impeding his vision, he had no warning before the front end of the car came to a sudden halt against a tree. The airbag exploded in his face. Everything was quiet now as the darkness overcame him.

Long Walk

With one large gasp for air, Jack sat bolt upright and put his hand to his head to feel for injuries. He was lying some ten feet from the car, his bag a few feet away. Checking for signs of blood, he found he was fairly clean aside from the dirt and debris clinging to his shirt and pants. Miraculously, it seemed, he had escaped serious injury. The car was a different story, however. Following the impact, he had run far off the road.

The vehicle sat lodged against the tree deep in the woods that lined the highway. The large buck had been crushed. The bloody mess appeared to be pushed into the front seat. This was definitely a setback to his timetable. Rolling to his knees, he reached for his bag. He was going to walk to the nearest house or business and call for a taxi or some other service to take him the last few miles to the hospice. He was sure that Sarah lay counting down her final moments, unaware that he was on his way to see her.

Brushing himself off, he began walking. A thick fog had settled in, and it imparted an eerie feel to the cool night air. It seemed he was utterly alone. His skin was chilled, but as he walked, he began to pay less attention to his own discomfort. His mind was occupied with contemplation. He reviewed the life he had made for himself since he had last seen Sarah.

The year following graduation, he had hitchhiked around the country, sometimes catching a ride on a cheap travel bus. Wherever he had ended up, he found work. He would save enough cash to head out to his next destination. Along the way, he had met many interesting people from all walks of life, and each had left their mark on him in some way.

By the end of that year, he had returned to his family home and begun attending the local state college. Not long after he had graduated with a Bachelor's degree in design, he began to work for a small advertising agency. After several years of hard work, he was made a partner.

There was no time for women. His work became his mistress. He drifted in and out of relationships over the years, but no one ever measured up to the standard set by the woman he was about to see again, probably for the last time. He wondered if it was possible that, when he saw Sarah, he would realize that all of his memories of her had somehow been exaggerated over time. Was it unrealistic to believe she would look the same? When cancer takes a life, it doesn't leave much behind, does it?

Jack was smart enough to know that selective memory is common, especially when recalling past relationships. We want to remember things the way that we want to remember them. How could he think she would be as happy to see him, as he would be to see her? Maybe he only imagined that her heart, after all these years, still belonged to him, as his belonged to her. After all, she had been the one to move away.

"No, she was simply confused, maybe overwhelmed as her life began to unfold." Jack spoke aloud to bolster his resolve. He was beginning to think he must be crazy for making this superhuman effort to reach someone who had so clearly rejected him in the past, leaving all those years ago without even saying goodbye. Startled, his mind snapped back to the present as he sensed a shadow off to the side of the road.

The man had materialized from out of the mist and stood leaning against a light pole with his black fedora tilted slightly to cover his eyes. "Ain't love somethin'?" He was grinning at Jack as he added, "Women get us to do the heavy work, travel thousands of miles, even kill our best mate. I mean, what does it take to get us to sacrifice everything? Did you ever think about how many wars have been fought over a woman?"

He pushed the brim of his hat up just enough to reveal his eyes. They seemed to burn through the fog and darkness toward him. "A flash of leg, the swish and sway of a perfect ass, all dressed up in six-inch heels. All we need is a sexy smile, and we're no better than animals in heat."

"What are you talking about? It wasn't like that with Sarah." Jack protested even as he wondered to himself why he should answer the strange man. "I've loved her since I was six years old. If she was the type of woman you describe, why would I bother to go see her at all?"

"My point exactly. Maybe you're just fooling yourself." The man grinned wide, "You're not a bad catch, but you fed on her bait until you were thirteen. That's when she set the hook, right before that summer with Granny. When she knew she had you for good, she didn't want you anymore. Right?"

"Wait! How would you know about that?" Jack squinted, trying to get a better look at the man's face. Perhaps it was someone from his past. He moved closer, but suddenly it dawned on him that something strange was going on. Hadn't he just taken several steps toward the man? Yet it seemed he was no closer at all.

"I know all of it, my friend. Sooner or later, we all have to face our demons. Question is, will you know yours when they come for you?" With that, the man tipped his hat again, winked, and walked away into the mist.

Jack rubbed his eyes with his free hand. "I must have landed harder than I thought!" When he looked again, there was nothing there. His mind was searching for a face that matched the stranger's. He shook his head.

The guy had been right about one thing. During the old days, and maybe even now, he would have sacrificed almost anything to be with Sarah. Especially if he thought there was a snowball's chance in hell she'd have had him. Engulfed in the misty morning, walking and still pondering the bizarre events of the night, it seemed no time at all before he arrived at his destination.

Arrival

Jack stood in the doorway, his heart pounding in his chest. Across the room, Sarah lay asleep. Gone was the vibrant girl he had last seen at the end of their eleventh grade. Here was a woman facing the last days of her life, a life he had never had the privilege of sharing. Whatever her past joys or sorrows, they were all irrelevant now. He was overcome with a deep sorrow at the sight of her, here alone.

Her room was decorated like any average bedroom in any average home. The walls were covered with a colorful floral paper, and there were a couple of framed pictures hanging, serene country images. Two table lamps sat on small tables on either side of her bed, a television hung from the wall in the corner, and a chair completed the decor. Despite the obvious effort to create a homey atmosphere, it seemed to Jack a sterile environment devoid of any real personality. The smell of chemical sanitizers hung heavy in the air, and it hurt his heart to think that this would be the last place her eyes would ever see, the last experience of her life.

He felt tired all of a sudden and sat in the chair, pulling it close to her bed. He detected a faint scent of impending death as he placed his bag on the floor next to him. Undoubtedly, the room had been shared by many who had lived their final moments here, winding down like a clock at the end of its battery until ultimately coming to rest.

"It doesn't have to be this way, does it?" Jack looked up at the ceiling and whispered his heartfelt plea. Was he asking God? "Isn't there some way to pull her back?" Of course, he knew that no one gets to choose how or when we leave this life. Jack shook his head. He was overcome.

As his mind went blank, a new thought wiggled its way in. Maybe he couldn't stop what was happening to Sarah, but he could at least brighten the time she had left. He pulled the chair closer to her bed and began to speak softly in the hushed tone that lovers often use.

Reunion

"Sarah?" He leaned in close, hoping not to startle her. She lay with her eyes closed offering no sign that she had heard him. He touched her hair and tried again a little louder. "Sarah, can you hear me?" Taking her hand, he was startled at how cold she was.

At the touch of his hand, her eyes fluttered open. "What?" She struggled to focus on his face, and he could see that she was having difficulty. "Glasses..." Ah, yes. He remembered her glasses. Even when they were very young, she had worn them. He spotted them now on her table, one of the metal earpieces poking out from beneath a tissue. Handing them to her, he sat back in the chair again.

"Thanks." Her hands shook as she awkwardly placed the spectacles on the bridge of her nose. She paused to look at him, studying him for a long time. His pulse began to thump in his ears as he willed her to recognize him, but she didn't seem to remember. Just as he was about to reveal himself to her, she touched his face.

"Jack?" She smiled. "Is that you? God, I hope... I'm not seeing things again." Her voice was weak and strained as she paused between each phrase gathering her strength.

"No... I mean yes. It really is me, Sarah. How are you?" *Why was he asking such a silly question? It was pretty damned obvious how she was.* A knot formed in his throat, and he felt the tears well up in his eyes.

"I'm fine. I have everything I need here." She coughed. "You look good, Jack. A little bit pale maybe, but it's so nice to see you." She took a deep breath before going on. "You should get out in the sun more." She smiled at him and reached out to take his hand.

He swallowed, forcing his throat to relax enough to speak. "Art got in touch with me. He told me what you have been going through. I wanted to see you before..." He realized what he was about to say and felt embarrassed. *What's my problem?*

"Before I *die*? It's okay... Jack, you can say it. I'm not afraid to talk about it." He believed her. She did seem to be at peace.

"What I was going to say is that I wanted to see you before you leave me again. I've tried to find you over the years, you know. I couldn't believe that you left all those years ago without saying goodbye."

"I'm sorry, Jack." She looked as though she really meant it. "My father got a new job that summer... We had to move right away... I didn't have time to say goodbye."

Jack nodded and gave her hand a little squeeze. "It's okay, Sarah. Art told me he followed you when you moved, and that you and he ended up getting married."

"Yes... He was attending college... After two years... we got married... When did you talk to him?"

"He called me yesterday to tell me where you were. We don't have to talk. I'm sorry. You were resting when I came in."

She shook her head, and went on. "Things didn't end so well with Art and me. He always accused me of... thinking about you."

"He mentioned something like that. Too bad, sometimes our imagination can get the best of us. It's like..."

"No, Jack," she interrupted. "It wasn't his imagination... I did think about you a lot. I even tried therapy a couple of times... to try to get you out of my head. Poor Art." She reached up to touch his face again. "Truth be told, I didn't want to stop thinking about you."

At that, he felt his eyes begin to well up again. With a tear running down his cheek, he confessed, "I... I never stopped thinking about you either. I used to fantasize what life could have been – what it might have been like if we had ended up together."

"Did you ever figure out... why it didn't work out? that you scared me? You were so...

intense." She fell silent for a moment, and he didn't know what to say. Finally, she looked up and smiled. "Remember the year... we were in that school play together? You carried me through the stage door?"

"Yeah, I always enjoyed those plays. I forgot about carrying you though. How could I forget that?"

"Well, you did... I have the scar to prove it." She lifted her arm to show him an inch-long scar near her elbow. "You picked me up and ran through the door... you scraped my elbow... against the doorframe... From that day on, I had a constant reminder... You scarred me for life." She coughed as she chuckled.

"I had forgotten that, honest, but thanks for reminding me." Even though she was horribly ill, he loved the way the little lines around her eyes made her look lovelier than ever. "I was clumsy back then and probably tripped over something. Okay, I'm making excuses. We were lucky I didn't fall completely. It might have been broken bones instead of a scraped arm." He started to laugh, but caught himself. "Anyway, sorry about that."

"Don't feel bad. It was like... having your name tattooed on my arm. It looks a little like a J... if you squint your eyes just right... and look at it from an angle."

"It does, doesn't it?" He was still looking at the scar when the nurse came into the room.

"How we doin' tonight, honey?"

Jack moved out of the way to give her some room. Sarah nodded and stared straight ahead as the nurse walked over to the side of the bed to check the IV drip, pushing a few buttons. Taking the clipboard from the side of the cart, she made a few notes before leaving the room as quietly as she had entered.

"Not much for conversation, is she?" Jack was at her bedside again and took her hand.

"I think she got the message." Sarah squeezed his hand.

"Message?"

"Couldn't you tell?" She was whispering. "I was willing her to hurry up and leave the room... I want to have time with you alone before..."

"I know, I know. Me too," was all he could say.

Take Me Away

Sarah closed her eyes as if trying to recall a distant memory. "Remember... you used to make up those wild stories... why I should be with you... how good our life could be?"

"Yes, I remember." He was embarrassed that *she* remembered that of all things. "I was trying too hard to get you to fall in love with me. I guess the story thing was kinda lame."

"No, Jack. Some were very nice... some were a little strange... I mean, sorry... not strange really... I felt like I was on a rollercoaster... your wild ideas... That's what scared me, I think."

"My stories scared you?"

"I think I was worried... you were too much of a dreamer... You know what I mean?" She patted his arm. "Mostly, I was afraid... your feelings for me... They were just too strong."

"Sarah... My feelings for you were too deep for my own good, and the stories weaved in bits and pieces of my hopes and dreams for us. I guess some of them were a bit over the top."

"We were young... and foolish... Today those stories might be nice to hear... You could turn them into a book... after I'm... gone."

"Well, I always felt I could write something, but where would I go with it? And, there never seems to be enough time." He stood up and gazed out of the small window as he spoke. The glow of streetlights lit up the water-stained glass and the shadows speckled across his face. "I guess some dreams are never meant to be."

The room fell silent. He was trying to remember the stories he had told, while Sarah was remembering how he used to push her on the backyard swing when they were eight years old. Soon she drifted off to sleep. Then suddenly, she opened her eyes again.

"Jack, tell me a story." She struggled to push herself up to a seated position. She reached for the control that dangled from the side of her bed, and pulled it up so she could push one of the buttons on the small box. The bed began to rise to support her from behind. He came to her bedside and gently tucked the covers around her slim body.

"I haven't told a story like that for years, Sarah."

"Imagine again, what our life could have been... if we had been together through those years? If everything had worked out... the way you used to want it? Tell me that story, Jack." She rested her head on her pillow and waited.

Had she seen into his soul? Did she know how often he had thought about it over the years?

"It's kind of sad when things don't turn out the way we planned. Most of us never get to live the life we dream." He looked into her eyes, and found new inspiration. "I can tell you our story, Sarah, but I'll be honest with you. I'm baring my soul here. These have been my thoughts and dreams for a long time, and I'll only share them with you if you promise not to laugh at me."

He crossed his heart with his hand, and she let out a wheezy laugh. Playfully, he gave her a stern look, and said, "You gotta promise now, or I'll never get through it. It takes a bit of concentration to put it all together. Sometimes my dreams are, er, um, a glimpse of ecstasy." He winked at her and raised his eyebrows, giving her a sly smile.

"Really, Jack Bailey!" Ah, now he had made her smile. "You haven't had visions of us having...? We never even got close... when we were together."

"I don't require the actual experience to think about what it could be like. I have a good imagination, remember?"

"And what could it be like, then?" Sarah's voice sounded the tiniest bit stronger. She was playing with him.

"Nice... I guess." Was he blushing? His face didn't feel warm, but he was sure it must be red.

"Just nice? Not all hot and steamy... like in the movies? Not all groaning... and tearing off each other's clothes? Rolling around on the bed? Really, Jack?"

"Is that how you would have wanted it? Because I could..."

"Well, no... not exactly, Mr. Fantasy..." She *was* playing with him. "I like it slow and gentle... Slow and gentle can still be hot... don't you think?"

"Yes, I think. You want me to tell a story, or do you want to talk about sex? 'Cause I'd be perfectly happy to..."

She smiled. "Tell the story, Jack. I was just teasing."

He smiled back at her and placed his hand on her forehead as though uploading his vision directly to her brain. "Okay, Sarah. Close your eyes now, and come away with me." She did as she was told. He leaned in and began talking softly, hypnotically, into her ear.

The Picnic

The house was set on the side of a gently sloping mountain. It had been built more than thirty years ago, but it was a beauty, so comfortable, and decorated just the way you like it. We had only been married for a few months when we moved in. You were so excited as we carried in our boxes. You literally danced around the living room. It made me laugh.

This morning you've been cleaning the kitchen as you prepared my favorite meal, while I've been out raking the yard. Since it is late spring, I am cleaning up the remnants of winter debris. The weather is warm, but the cool breezes coming down from the melting snow on the mountain feel good to me as I work. Around lunchtime, you come out the back door and stand on the small porch.

You look amazing, by the way, with your long red skirt billowing out to the side, and your white sweater buttoned all the way up. You know, the one with the small pockets meant to cover your nipples and keep them from poking out whenever you are cold. Did you know that when the first cold breeze came along, I could see them anyway?

Sarah instinctively pulled up her covers and poked him in the ribs with her free hand. Ignoring her, he went on...

You had a picnic basket in one hand and a blanket draped over your arm. When you realized you had my attention, you called, "Are you ready for some lunch?"

I smiled at you and dropped the rake immediately. See what you do to me? I'm like a schoolboy. "Looks like we're having a picnic," I say.

"I was hoping we could go up the slope."

How could I say no? I would have climbed Mount Everest to see you smile that way.

Sarah interrupted, "Where do we live? It sounds so nice. Tell me more about it before we go on the picnic."

"Well," Jack started, as he sat down on the edge of the bed next to her.

Our house overlooked a blue lake nestled between the mountains. From our front porch, we could watch the deer as they made their way to the water each morning. Grand old trees lined the sloping hills surrounding the valley, and when the fog would roll in, they reminded us of sentinels keeping watch over the top of the mist.

Behind our house, the upward slope was covered in tall spring grass and an occasional boulder broke up the smooth field of waving green. As we walk up the hill, we are holding hands, and I can feel your vibrant spirit and warmth, like energy from the sun flowing into me. Every time I look over at you, you are looking back at me. Your broad smile always makes me smile back, and I start to think that this is what heaven must be like.

Halfway to the large tree where we will set up our picnic, you stop and pull yourself into me. We stand there holding each other, and you say, "Look at our beautiful world, Jack. It's everything I ever dreamed."

I kiss the top of your head and answer, "I know. We'll have to struggle for a while, but this view, being here with you, makes everything worth it."

You hug me even more tightly and share what's been on your mind for weeks. "It's so much more than the view. Don't you think it's the perfect time to start our family?" There you are, looking up at me with those eyes of yours sparkling and bright.

"Oh, absolutely!" I kiss you again with great excitement. You take my hand and pull me toward our favorite picnic spot. Slightly out of breath, you hand me the blanket. It unfurls as I spread it over the tall grass. You kneel down to press it flat against the ground, and then hold your arms out, beckoning me to join you.

We open the basket, and you pull out a couple of sandwiches. There's a bottle of wine, but something is wrong. You frantically search the basket and frown as you tell me, "I forgot the wine glasses!" I respond by opening the bottle and drinking straight from it. You look shocked. I laugh. "Tilt your head back," I say.

You indulge my silliness and gulp thirstily as I pour until you finally hold your hand up to signal you've had enough. Wiping the dribble from your lips, you look like a little girl who has just enjoyed a cookie sneaked from the cupboard.

"Remember when I used to take a couple of freshly baked cookies from my mom's kitchen?" Jack stopped for a moment to ask Sarah the question. Her eyes still closed, she smiled and nodded.

"Go on with the story, Jack," she urged.

You snatch the bottle of wine from my hand and tell me, "It's your turn." I wonder if you will go easy on me or pour too much and spill it all over me, but carefully you pour the Shiraz as I drink as much as I can. Handing the bottle back to me, you choose your sandwich while I stand the bottle against the basket. You had wrapped our sandwiches in white paper and now you are slowly unwrapping one to keep the best bits from falling out. Holding it out for me, you ask, "Bite?" and I do. The flavors are familiar, but that sandwich is just about the best thing I have ever tasted. Was it the food, or the moment? I can't be sure. You take a smaller bite, and continue to share it with me until the sandwich is gone.

We take turns sipping the wine until it is half spent and standing back in the corner of the basket. Gobbling down the next sandwich as if it were our last meal, we talk and laugh together between bites. We wash down the final crumbs as we empty the wine bottle, and pack up to go. We are always careful not to leave anything behind.

"Am I tipsy?" you ask.

"You look a little tipsy. Your nose looks happy!" I reach out and touch it. "I don't think you've ever drunk half a bottle of wine in one sitting before."

We lean back and look up at the sky, taking in the day. The sun is warm on our faces. Turning to face each other, we prop ourselves up on our elbows. Funny, how we can enjoy the simple pleasure of just gazing into each other's eyes. The sun is shining through your hair, the breeze causing it to frame your face, and I think you are the most beautiful woman in the world.

I move to kiss you but you roll away, repositioning yourself on your back, teasing me to come closer. Your breasts rise and fall with every breath and my desire is growing. Leaning toward you, I am thrilled when you stretch up to place your lips on mine. The kiss is long and passionate. My heart is beating faster as you reach down and catch hold of my belt...

"Oh really, Jack? You really thought about this, didn't you?" Sarah brought him back to the present. He had been experiencing the most delightful trance as he was telling the story.

"Well, let me just say, if I could have planned our life together, this is exactly what I would have wanted it to look like."

"Of course you would, and it was such a nice scenario. Do we end up making love up there?"

"Uh, well, yeah, if you let me finish the story..."

"Hmmm... I'm feeling a little tired. Is it okay if I savor the fantasy while I close my eyes for a few minutes?"

"Sure. I'll cue up the next story while you rest." He bent over her and kissed her forehead before sitting back in the chair next to the bed. He noticed it was still dark outside and thought to himself that this night was magic. It seemed to go on forever. He closed his eyes to rest, but sleep did not come.

Family

Startled, he opened his eyes to see Sarah sitting up in the bed She was coughing. "Are you okay?" He stood and gently rubbed her back.

"I'm fine, Jack. It might sound strange but... I'm feeling better somehow." She grinned up at him. "You think I got a little sexual healing from that last part?"

"Well, wouldn't that be a good reason for making love? I hear it has health benefits!"

"Easy, cowboy. We're in a hospice, not a hostel. Let's save it for a suite at the Ritz." She brushed some stray hairs from her face. "Got any more stories? Maybe the next one will make my headache go away."

"In fact, I do, and this one will expound upon the fruits of our labors back there on the hill."

"You and your flowery language. I could fall big for such a scholar!" She giggled.

Jack remembered that sound. How he'd missed the girl of his childhood. Now he felt he was on the right track. If he had failed to win her heart when they were young, he was succeeding now. The next story was much closer to his heart. He hoped he wouldn't choke up as he told it.

"Are you ready then?"

"Whenever you are, I have nowhere else I'd rather be..."

She lay back against the pillow again and waited as he cleared his throat.

> Our son was born a mere eight and a half months after that picnic. He was a healthy and feisty little guy from the first moment he arrived. We enjoyed him so much that we were elated when his sister arrived three years later. She was such a happy baby.
>
> Now, many years after that picnic on the hill, we continue to feel blessed. God must have taken the best bits from both of us. Our children are beautiful, intelligent, and very well behaved.

"What did we name them?"

He thought for a moment before turning it back to her. "What names would you have liked?"

"How about Bartholomew and Evelyn?"

"Are you serious? Bartholomew? Bart Bailey?"

"I think that is a strong sounding name, don't you?" She grinned.

"Uh... it sounds a lot like a circus to me."

"Well, we might need to negotiate some on the names, Mr. Storyteller, but do go on. Tell me more."

He thought for a moment and continued...

It's Christmas Eve, and we've just finished dinner. It was your idea to put on the holiday music. The soft sound playing in the background adds just the right spirit as we carry the plates full of special holiday foods to the table.

Before you ask what we were eating, let me tell you. There was honey-roasted ham sliced on the platter, cold boiled shrimp with cocktail sauce – one of my favorites. There's a very festive potato salad with multi-colored vegetables, broccoli quiche casserole, and some other dishes that you always make. You call them your favorite family traditions.

The children were wiggling in their seats because, just in the other room, the Christmas tree is glowing and beckoning to them with tinsel laden outstretched branches.

"If it's okay with you, I'm going to use my names for the children."

"Oh sure, I see how it is. Do you always get your way, Mr. Storyteller?" She pretended to be annoyed, but he saw through it. He leaned closer to her and softly stroked her hair.

"Anyway..."

Michael is eight years old this Christmas, and Lauren is five. We've finally given them permission to leave the table and they are running for the great room where that magnificent tree reaches to the ceiling. The gifts are beautifully wrapped, and you have topped each one with curled ribbons and bows. Hidden among them are two bicycles, a doll for Lauren, little robots and a model car for Michael. There are games and puzzles, a paint-by-number set, and books, lots of books. Oh, but wait... let's back up a minute...

As always, setting up the tree was a family event. We hiked up the mountain, with Lauren riding on the sled. You and the children selected just the right one from among the many young pines. I cut it down while you reminded them how we will plant another young tree in the spring to take its place and keep the forest alive.

After pulling the tree home on the sled, we supervised the kids as they carefully hung each ornament, occasionally stopping for a sip of hot cocoa and a bite of a Christmas cookie. Finally, we topped it with a silver star that was a gift from your mother, an heirloom from your grandmother. It's the perfect touch.

Afterward, with a fire to warm us, we watched reruns of those old holiday shows we grew up watching. Though we've seen them a dozen times before, they still make us smile. Lauren calls to us from the window. "Look! It's snowing!" Michael runs to see if it's so, and soon we are all standing at the window.

"The large flakes will be perfect for Santa's sleigh," you tell them. Michael gives you a knowing look, but doesn't spoil it for his sister. I think back a couple of years ago, how we were a bit sad when he discovered the truth about Santa.

You read "The Night before Christmas" while I sit with my arms around them, one on each side. I love hearing your voice as you make the story come alive. Lauren claps when you are finished. Then, we hang our stockings by the chimney *with care*. You stand back and declare, "Everything is ready."

"Wait!" Michael wants to set out some cookies for Santa. He winks at us and tells Lauren, "Santa gets hungry because he has to work all night." She helps him arrange the plate and glass of milk on the table by the tree.

"It's time to go to bed now," I tell them. "Santa can't come if you're awake." They scramble up the stairs, and I follow them to tuck them in their beds. You come up to say goodnight and listen to their prayers before turning off the lights. We are sure they will lay awake for hours with their Christmas flashlights, the ones they found in their stockings last year.

You head down to the kitchen to clean up while I go to the attic. I bring out a few gifts we had hidden there. When I come downstairs, you are waiting for me with something a bit stronger than cocoa. You give me that look and a grin, telling me, "Something to warm us up and get us going."

There are still a few gifts to wrap, however, and we spend our time cutting and taping rather than romping on the couch. When it's finally time to go to go to bed, we are both so tired that we agree that we better get some rest. "We can play another time," you say, and I agree.

Ah, but then I go and mess things up. I start touching you that way. You know, the way you can't resist. In a moment, you are taking those short breaths that tell me I'm right.

Jack paused a moment, taking a deep breath. He had been whispering that last part very close to Sarah's ear. He closed his eyes and kissed the top of Sarah's head, breathing in the smell of her hair before continuing, "Thirty minutes later, we finally lay down to rest."

Jack had always been blessed with a vivid imagination, but it was no exaggeration to say that he was actually experiencing the story as he spun the tale for her. It made him feel alive again with an energy he had been missing for some time. He hoped it didn't sound crazy when he confessed as much to Sarah.

"Wow. That was good. Does it seem strange for me to say I felt as though it were really happening? I wouldn't want to scare you." He winked at her then.

"Well, this may sound even stranger. I feel so much better after that story," she admitted.

"You mean better about us?"

"No, Jack, I mean I feel better, as in stronger, healthier."

"Good medicine, eh?"

"Really, I'm serious. I haven't felt this good in months." Her eyes were clear, like pools of liquid emerald. "Tell me another one, please?"

"Don't you want to take a break, maybe, for a few minutes?"

"No. I want you to tell me a story right now and make it a good one! Let's see what another dose of your medicine can do."

"How can I say no to that? Let me think, hmm. I don't just carry stories around in my head."

"Oh, really? It seems to me like you've been thinking about these stories for some time, Jack Bailey. Tell me the most romantic one. Tell me the one you think about when you're alone in your bed, in the dark."

"What makes you think I think about you in bed?" He knew he was blushing.

She let out a laugh. "Because I can't tell you how many times I have dreamed about you. I knew how much you loved me when we were young, Jack. A love like that never dies. Even when people are thousands of miles apart, a love like that can survive and grow. I wouldn't be surprised if it even transcends death."

"Damn, woman! I wish you wouldn't use the "D" word. I can't wrap my head around it. Besides, I don't know if I can bear losing you again... forever."

"Listen, Jack, I don't think I'm wrong about enduring love. Let me tell *you* a story."

To America

When I was a little girl, I used to spend two weeks at my grandmother's house every other summer. They lived on a slope at the foot of a mountain, almost like the one you dreamt for us. I was surprised one year when she told me the story of how they came to live there.

In 1908, they were living in Wales where my grandfather worked in the coalmines. Even though he worked more than twelve hours a day, six days a week, they lived in a very small home. You might even call it a shack. It was owned by the coal company.

My grandmother wanted to start a family, but Grandpa resisted. He told her that they should save any money they could and use it to go to America. He believed that in America they would have a chance at a better life.

In the winter of 1910, they bought a ticket for one. It was all they could afford with the small amount of money they had been able to save. They planned for my grandfather to come here and find work, while Nana moved back in with her family. Grandpa would send for her after he got settled. They were very excited about the possibilities for their future.

Because he was a coal miner, when he landed at Ellis Island, my grandfather was given a choice of two locations where he could go. Back then, you know, you had to let them know what kind of work you could do in order to be allowed into our country. If you had no skills, you could be forced to return to your home country.

He chose to travel to Pennsylvania where he found work in the mines. After two years, he combined what was left of the money he had brought with him, and what he had saved from working long hours at the mine, and bought a small plot of land. With the help of his friends from the mine, my grandfather built a tidy little house.

Because telephones were a luxury back then, the only way they could communicate was by writing letters. Nana told me that she would hear the sound of Grandpa's voice as she read his letters, and he would do the same with hers. That way, it was as though they were having a real conversation. Only with very long pauses, if you know what I mean.

It was the spring of 1912, when my grandmother finally set sail to be with the love of her life. Three months later, she joined him in their new home, at the foot of a mountain overlooking a valley with a lake.

"I don't remember if I ever told you that story before, but you can see now that the house you described in that first story sounded almost exactly like my Nana's house." Sarah paused. He smiled at her, but before he could say a word, she began again.

"Anyway, as a young girl, I often imagined what love could be like. When I was around twelve years old, I read several classic love stories. I thought something like that could only be true in fairy tales. However, it was during my next visit that Nana let me read the letters. She had stacks of them. They were sorted by date and tied in bundles for every season of the years they were apart. Love letters like that are seldom written anymore. With cell phones and computers, there are so many ways to communicate now. The art of the love letter may be lost forever."

She appeared a little flushed. "I think I'm rambling."

"No, you're doing just fine. I didn't know any of that about your family. My grandfather was a coal miner, too."

"Really? We have always had so much in common. I can't believe I didn't see it before."

"Please, go ahead and finish telling me about the letters. Are you feeling okay?"

She nodded and continued, "For the next couple of days, I read page after page of my grandfather's words. Sometimes I could hear him talking in his raspy old voice as I read. I tried to imagine what he must have been like when he was younger. When I finally finished the last letter, I felt I had discovered what it really means to know love. I was on a mission, after that, to find a love that resembled what my grandparents had known. After a while, I couldn't believe that a guy like that even existed in our town."

"Maybe there was someone, but because you were with him every day, he became too familiar."

"You mean you, Jack?" She smiled at him as she asked. It threw him off guard. He didn't know where she was going with that question.

"Uh, well, of course, I was hoping."

"Tell me another story, and I'll let you know how I really feel."

"Promise?"

"Promise."

Caribbean Dream

We were very dedicated to our kids, you know. Shuttling them to baseball practice and dancing lessons, Cub Scouts and Brownies meetings, we watched with pride as they grew and matured. The day finally came when first Michael, and then Lauren went off to college. We squeezed each other tight and said our prayers for them. We realized that we would no longer be there to protect them from the world.

The house was much quieter, but we were learning to enjoy our new freedom to be together again, just you and me. We often took our coffee out to the porch at the end of the day, and spent time looking back on our wonderful life. One day, when we were reminiscing about all the family vacations we had taken when the kids were younger, we recalled the fun we'd had at the Grand Canyon and Niagara Falls. From the Grand Tetons to Mammoth Caves, each year we had chosen a new destination. We had driven everywhere with the children, singing songs and sharing great family moments together, but we had never set aside time for a vacation just for us.

So we planned a trip to a tropical paradise. It was to be a seven-day adventure. We spent a lot of time eating, talking, and relaxing in hammocks as tall drinks, embellished with tiny umbrellas and plastic swords laden with olives, were brought to us on a tray. Best of all, we enjoyed romping in the large Jacuzzi that came with our room.

Every day, we tried something new. We went snorkeling on the reef, horseback riding in the surf, and even floated down an underground river on small round rubber rafts. We finally had the opportunity to enjoy ourselves in an exotic place. There was no schedule, and nothing to worry over.

Early in the evening, after one of the most amazing seafood dinners we had ever enjoyed, we took a walk on the beach to watch the sun set. As anyone who frequents the beach knows, there can be scattered rain clouds one minute, and in the next, it can be dry and beautiful again. There had been some of those scattered showers as we dined, but as we walked, the rays of sun lit up the bright blue tones of the perfect ocean scene.

We had talked about how we had put off such a trip until the kids were grown. We were happy to have done so, but we wondered if we could have chosen a better way when it came to some other things. We agreed, then, on a pact to let go of any second thoughts and live completely in the moment.

"Don't worry, Sarah," I told you, as we faced the water. "Let your regrets wash away into the sea. Instead of looking back, let's move forward and make the next phase the best time of our lives." You take my hand as we walk down the shoreline, occasionally stopping to pick up a colorful shell. As I stood up from retrieving a perfect little sea sponge from the flotsam, we catch each other's eyes.

Jack stopped. "Oh, Sarah, those eyes. I am still so taken with you."

Sarah looked up at him then, and he could see that she had been a little teary. Without a word, she squeezed his hand. He felt as though his heart would break, and yet he was strangely elated. At last, she broke the silence. "Go on," she managed to whisper.

He took a deep breath. "Where was I?" he asked. "Oh yes, those eyes..."

Looking into those eyes draws me into a thousand moments of joy, and hope. I pull you to me and wrap my arms tightly around you. The waves are crashing and washing over our feet as I plant an epic kiss on your sweet lips.

When we finally release each other, you catch your breath and point out over the ocean. The sun is beginning to slip low in the horizon leaving a golden sky filled with something neither of us had ever seen. A full double rainbow arced across the sky before us, touching down on the surface of the sea. I hug you to my side as we marvel at the magic of the moment. It's like a promise that no matter what life may have in store for us, we will be together, and everything will be okay.

"That's the story you should have told me in eighth grade." She whispered, wiping a single tear from her cheek. Still, she was smiling.

"You think that would have made the difference?"

"Jack, if you had told me these stories back then, I may have laughed at you at the time, but over time, it would have made a future together seem possible."

"You don't know how many times I wished I had told you what I really felt deep inside. If only you could have known what I knew, that we were destined to be together forever." He smiled and made his voice sound light. He wasn't trying to overwhelm her with his intensity - again.

"Forever is a long time, Jack, but I think I'd like to give it a try. I have to tell you, I wasn't well at all before you came here. I think I was done fighting the inevitable, but now, I feel even better than I did before I got sick." She sat up as if to get out of her bed. "Look, it's daylight. I don't even remember seeing the sun rise."

Jack turned to see the bright white light pouring through the window. "Wow, look at that. It's a *very* sunny day!"

"I haven't been out in the sunshine for such a long time. Do you think we could go for a walk?" She moved her legs closer to the edge of the bed.

"Do you really feel up to it? Maybe you should try to stand first and we'll see how that goes."

She smiled at him as he stood and took her hand. He stiffened his arms to help her steady herself and pulled gently to give her a lift. Something wasn't right. She seemed a little too heavy for her tiny body. Were the blankets on the bed caught on something? Suddenly, as if something had let go, she sat all the way up and swung her feet to the floor. He gasped. She stood before him in her thin nightgown, and his heart was taken by her once more.

"Jack, I feel so light and happy. It's as if you healed me."

"I feel the same way. I can't remember the last time I felt so good."

She was radiant as the light in the room restored the youthful beauty to her face. Holding out her hand, she said, "Let's go take that walk."

He reached out to steady her, but instead, she put her arm around him. He put his arm around her and kissed her.

"This feels so natural." She tilted her head a little to rest lightly on his shoulder. "It feels like... home!" Her voice sounded almost airy.

"Yes, it's... like a dream." He closed his eyes and relished the feeling. When he opened them, he spotted a door. He hadn't realized it was there before then. "Does that door take us outside?"

"I'm not sure. Maybe it does. I guess I've been too sick to notice it there before." She took a step toward it and stopped again. "That door looks familiar for some reason."

"How so?"

"Well, the way the glass is divided by the crossbars... and the curtain... it looks... it looks like the back door from my Nana's house! Outside that door was her garden... she always had such a beautiful garden."

"That's weird, Sarah, but really kind of nice at the same time." He gave her a squeeze. When they reached the door, Jack turned the knob. It swung open easily, as though on its own. The bright warm white light enveloped them.

When they stepped out together, it was just as Sarah had described. They entered a courtyard full of exotic flowers and perfectly pruned trees. It felt as though they were floating. The music in the air seemed to flow through them, a soft and beautiful song. The vibrantly colored flowers and lush green plants seemed to sway gently to its rhythm.

Sarah looked at Jack and smiled. She was thinking about something her grandmother had once said. "There shall be no more death, and no sorrow ..." Jack finished the thought, "...and neither shall there be any pain."

Closure

The nurse entered the room, speaking her usual quiet greeting. She checked the IV bag, and turned to her patient. Putting her fingers to Sarah's wrist, she checked for a pulse. She was warm to the touch, but there was no sign of life. She continued checking to be sure until, silently, she crossed her heart and bowed her head. "May God be with you on your journey home, Sarah. It will all be good now, no more suffering." With that, she pulled the blanket up to cover her smiling peaceful face.

A few miles away, the highway patrol officer had stopped. He had set out some flares after he followed the tire marks to discover the wrecked car off the highway and into the woods. He called in the accident and walked to the wreckage. There was a dead deer atop the front of the car. He picked up his pace as he called into dispatch one more time. "You got an ambulance on the way? There's somebody in here."

Through the driver's side window, he could see the bloodied man slumped over the steering wheel. There was no movement. He tried to open the door, but it was locked or likely jammed. Taking the baton from his belt, he rapped it hard against the glass.

"Come on!" he yelled. Finally, the window gave way, shattering into a thousand tiny diamonds that fell at his feet and across the man's lap. Reaching through the window, he put his fingers to the victim's neck checking for a pulse. The flesh was warm, but he was gone.

"Damn!" He jerked his hand back, wiped a small amount of blood from his fingers, and walked to the front of the car. It was nearly wrapped around the trunk the tree. He laid his hand on the hood. It was cold to the touch.

Back at the hospice, the nurse had finished moving the equipment out of Sarah's room while two men from the coroner's office loaded the body into the transport. Turning to leave the room, she noticed something lying on the floor next to the chair. It looked like some kind of duffle bag. She picked it up and sat it on the chair to look inside. As she unzipped the bag, she saw neatly folded clothes and some men's toiletries.

"Now that's a strange one. I don't remember anyone coming to visit in the last couple of days," she muttered as she carried it off to the lost and found closet.

"Whadda we got?" A second officer had arrived at the scene of the accident.

"He's gone." The first cop shook his head, "Poor bastard musta been alive in there for some time. He's still warm, but the engine's cold."

"Yeah, poor bastard is right." the other cop repeated.

"His GPS is still in there talking about "recalculating". Looks like he was headed over to the hospice just outside of town. Wonder who he was going to see."

"Doesn't matter anymore. They're probably together now. I'll call the coroner."

Small slips of pink paper dotted the ground around the wreck. As he walked back to his car, he bent and picked one up. In a child's handwriting, it read:

"See you at the playground ♥ *together forever."*

Author's Note

Thank you, dear reader, for taking this journey with me. Although this is a fictional tale, I took special inspiration from my life and weaved it throughout this story.

The mystery lies in identifying what is real and what is not. If you allow your imagination to carry you away, you will surely discover the secrets.